Traction Man Is Here!

MINI GREY

Dragonfly Books
New York

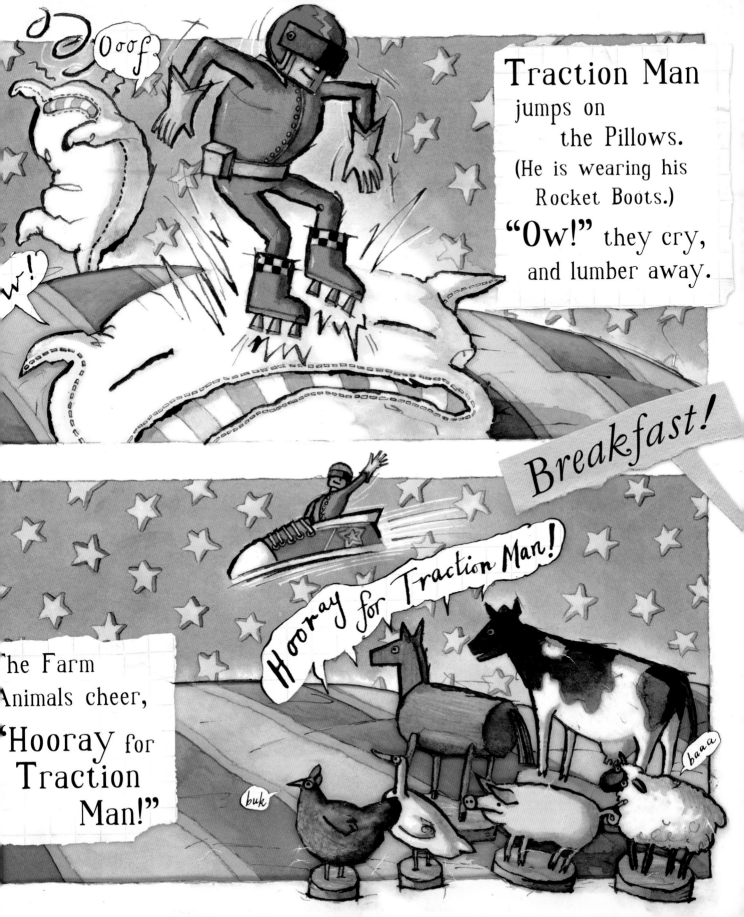

Traction Man is guarding some toast.

Now
who's going to help
with the washing up?

He volunteers for a Special Mission.

Traction Man is diving in the foamy waters
of the Sink (wearing his Sub-Aqua Suit,
Fluorescent Flippers, and Infra-Red Mask).

He is searching for the
Lost Wreck of the Sieve.

"Well done,
    Scrubbing Brush!
        You can be my pet!"

Just ten minutes, remember...

Traction Man is crawling through the overgrown shrubbery near the Pond, wearing Jungle Pants, Camouflage Vest and Sweaty Bandanna.

The Dollies have all been buried up to their waists in the flowerbed by Wicked Professor Spade.

"Oh, Traction Man, how can we repay you?"
"Think nothing of it, Ladies.
                    All in a day's work."

Traction Man and Scrubbing Brush are **deep, deep** down at the Bottom of the Bath. (Traction Man is wearing his Deep-Sea Diving Suit, Brass Helmet, and Metal Shoes.)

Somewhere down here, legend says, are the Mysterious Toes.

Oh, no! The Toes have suddenly appeared and have captured **Scrubbing Brush!**

Traction Man and Scrubbing Brush are in the Giant InterGalactic People Mover.

They are counting Christmas trees.

They are put into suspended animation for some of the journey.

At last!
Granny's!

Everyone has a present to open.
Even **Traction Man.**

ZOP!

B!M!

for Traction Man

Scrubbing Brush
is **very** excited.

Oh! How lovely (grrrr).
An all-in-one knitted green romper suit
and matching bonnet!

It is
a perfect
fit.

Traction Man
is speeding in his
Supersonic
Space-Cup
and Saucer
(wearing his all-in-one
knitted green romper suit
and matching bonnet)
on his way to rescue
the Cupcake from
the clutches of
Doctor Sock.

But—
Oh, no!

Well, at least Scrubbing Brush doesn't laugh at him.

Traction Man is sitting on the edge of the Kitchen Cliff
(wondering how long he will have to wear his all-in-one knitted
green romper suit and matching bonnet).

My goodness! Down there!
    All those Spoons have crashed! They must be helped—
but how? The Kitchen Cliff is very high.

Traction Man and **Scrubbing Brush**
are relaxing after their latest mission,
lying comfortably on a book
in the huge blue expanse
of the Carpet.

Traction Man is wearing his
knitted Green Swimming Pants
and matching Swimming Bonnet.

They are both wearing their medals.

And they know they are ready
for **Anything.**

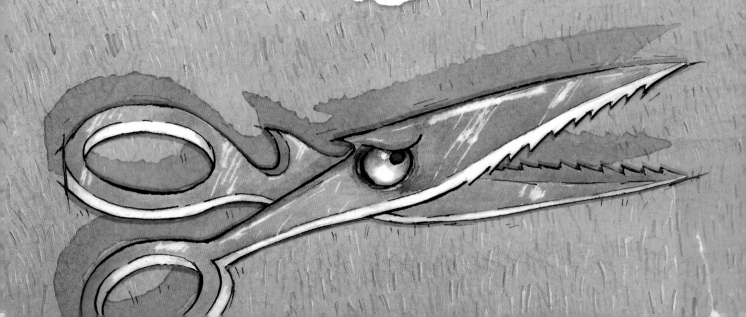

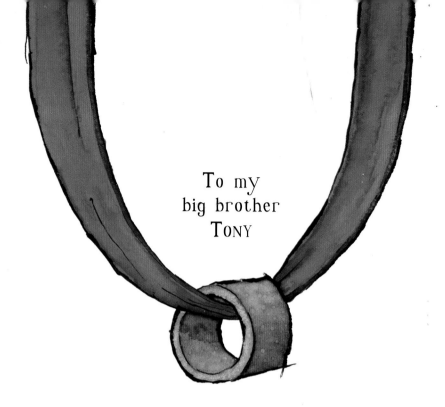

To my
big brother
TONY

All rights reserved. Published in the United States by Dragonfly Books, an imprint of
Random House Children's Books, a division of Random House, Inc., New York. Originally published
in hardcover in Great Britain by Jonathan Cape, an imprint of Random House Children's Books,
a division of the Random House Group Limited, London, and simultaneously published in the
United States by Alfred A. Knopf, an imprint of Random House Children's Books, in 2005.

Dragonfly Books with the colophon is a registered trademark of Random House, Inc.

Visit us on the Web! randomhouse.com/kids

Educators and librarians, for a variety of teaching tools, visit us at randomhouse.com/teachers

The Library of Congress has cataloged the hardcover edition of this work as follows:
Grey, Mini.
Traction Man is here! / by Mini Grey.
p. cm.
Summary: Traction Man, a boy's courageous action figure, has a variety of adventures with
Scrubbing Brush and other objects in the house.
ISBN 978-0-375-83191-1 (trade) — ISBN 978-0-375-93191-8 (lib. bdg.) —
ISBN 978-0-375-98701-4 (ebook)
[1. Action figures (Toys)—Fiction. 2. Toys—Fiction. 3. Brooms and brushes—Fiction.] I. Title.
PZ7.G873Tr 2005
[E]—dc22
2004004452

ISBN 978-0-307-93111-5 (pbk.)

Printed in China

10 9 8 7 6 5 4 3 2

First Dragonfly Books Edition